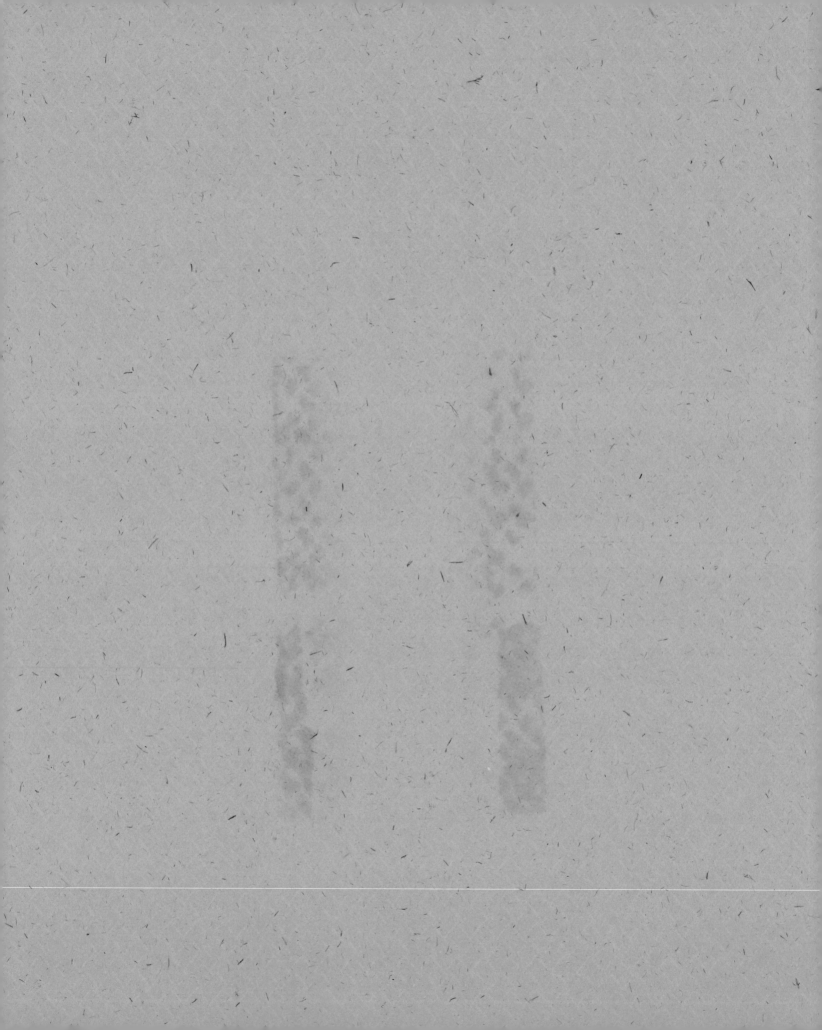

Aunt Pitty Patty's
PIGGY

Retold by Jim Aylesworth

Illustrated by Barbara McClintock

Scholastic Press · New York

LIBRARY OF CONGRESS CATALOGING-IN-PUBLICATION DATA

Aylesworth, Jim.
Aunt Pitty Patty's piggy / retold by Jim Aylesworth;
illustrated by Barbara McClintock.
p. cm.
Summary: A cumulative tale in which Aunt Pitty Patty's niece, Nelly,
tries to get piggy to go through the gate.
ISBN 0-590-89987-2
[1. Folklore.] I. McClintock, Barbara, ill. II. Title.
PZ8.1.A887Au 1999   398.22—dc21
[E] 98-46263   CIP   AC

10   9   8   7   6   5   4   3   2   1   9/9 0/0 01 02 03 04
Printed in the U.S.A.   37

FIRST EDITION, SEPTEMBER 1999
The display type was set in Callifonts 68 and Beffle.
The text type was set in 13 point ITC Esprit Medium.
The artwork was rendered in brown pencil and watercolor.
Book design by David Saylor

To Bill Martin Jr, with love!

—J. A.

To Dianne, with love

—B. M.

Once upon a time, Aunt Pitty Patty
took her little niece Nelly to the market.

While they were there,
Aunt Pitty Patty bought
a piggy.

It was a fine fat piggy, and together,
little Nelly and Aunt Pitty Patty led it home.

But when they got to the gate, the piggy would not go through it. Try what they may, the piggy would not budge. It just sat there sayin', **"No, no, no, I will not go!"**

At last, Aunt Pitty Patty said, "I can't fool with this piggy any longer! It's gettin' late and supper needs fixin'!"

So she sent little Nelly down the road to get some help.

And Aunt Pitty Patty went inside
to fix supper.

Little Nelly went down the road, and after a bit, she met a dog.
Little Nelly said, "Dog, dog, come bite Aunt Pitty Patty's piggy.
It's gettin' late, and piggy's by the gate sayin',
'No, no, no, I will not go!'"

But the dog wouldn't.

So little Nelly went a little farther, and she found a stick, and
she said, "Stick, stick, come hit dog. Dog won't bite Aunt Pitty
Patty's piggy. It's gettin' late, and piggy's by the gate sayin',
'No, no, no, I will not go!'"
But the stick wouldn't.

So little Nelly went a little farther, and she found a fire, and she said, "Fire, fire, come burn stick. Stick won't hit dog. Dog won't bite Aunt Pitty Patty's piggy. It's gettin' late, and piggy's by the gate sayin',

'No, no, no, I will not go!'"

But the fire wouldn't.

So little Nelly went a little farther, and she found
some water, and she said, "Water, water, come
douse fire. Fire won't burn stick. Stick won't hit dog.

Dog won't bite Aunt Pitty Patty's piggy. It's gettin'
late, and piggy's by the gate sayin',
        'No, no, no, I will not go!'"

But the water wouldn't.

So little Nelly went a little farther, and she found an ox, and she said, "Ox, ox, come drink water. Water won't douse fire. Fire won't burn stick. Stick won't hit dog. Dog won't bite Aunt Pitty Patty's piggy. It's gettin' late, and piggy's by the gate sayin',
'No, no, no, I will not go!'"
But the ox wouldn't.

So little Nelly went a little farther, and she found a butcher, and she said, "Butcher, butcher, come scare ox. Ox won't drink water. Water won't douse fire. Fire won't burn stick. Stick won't hit dog. Dog won't bite Aunt Pitty Patty's piggy. It's gettin' late, and piggy's by the gate sayin',

'No, no, no, I will not go!'"

But the butcher wouldn't.

ED'S MEATS

So little Nelly went a little farther, and she found a rope, and she said, "Rope, rope, come tie butcher. Butcher won't scare ox. Ox won't drink water. Water won't douse fire. Fire won't burn stick. Stick won't hit dog. Dog won't bite Aunt Pitty Patty's piggy. It's gettin' late, and piggy's by the gate sayin',

'No, no, no, I will not go!'"

But the rope wouldn't.

So little Nelly went a little farther, and she found a rat, and she said, "Rat, rat, come gnaw rope. Rope won't tie butcher. Butcher won't scare ox. Ox won't drink water. Water won't douse fire. Fire won't burn stick.

Stick won't hit dog. Dog won't bite Aunt Pitty Patty's piggy. It's gettin' late, and piggy's by the gate sayin',

'No, no, no, I will not go!'"

But the rat wouldn't.

So little Nelly went a little farther, and she met a cat, and she said, "Cat, cat, come chase rat. Rat won't gnaw rope. Rope won't tie butcher. Butcher won't scare ox. Ox won't drink water. Water won't douse fire. Fire won't burn stick. Stick won't hit dog. Dog won't bite Aunt Pitty Patty's piggy. It's gettin' late, and piggy's by the gate sayin',

'No, no, no, I will not go!'"

And the cat said, "If you will fetch me some milk, I will do it."

So little Nelly went a little farther, and she met a cow,
and she said, "Cow, cow, give me some milk."

And the cow said, "If you fetch me some hay, I will do it."

So little Nelly went a little farther, and she met Farmer Brown, and she said, "Farmer Brown, Farmer Brown, please give me some hay."

And Farmer Brown said, "Aren't you Aunt Pitty Patty's little niece Nelly?"

And little Nelly said, "Yes, I am."

And Farmer Brown said, "And where is your Aunt Pitty Patty right now?"

And little Nelly said, "She's fixin' supper."

And Farmer Brown said, "And what's for supper?"

And little Nelly said, "I don't know, but if you'll give me some hay, we can go and find out."

So Farmer Brown gave her some hay.

And little Nelly took the hay and gave it to the cow.

And when the cow had finished eating the hay,
she gave little Nelly some milk.

And little Nelly took the milk and gave it to the cat.

And when the cat had finished drinking the milk, he
began to chase the rat, and the rat began to the gnaw the
rope, and the rope began to tie the butcher, and the butcher
began to scare the ox, and the ox began to drink the water,

and the water began to douse the fire, and the fire began to
burn the stick, and the stick began to hit the dog, and the dog
began to bite the piggy. . . .

And the piggy went through the gate!

And Farmer Brown and little Nelly and
Aunt Pitty Patty all sat down to supper.